YOU'RE THE SCAREDY-CAT

For Gabby

McGraw-Hill
Children's Publishing
A Division of The **McGraw·Hill** Companies

Send all inquiries to: McGraw-Hill Children's Publishing • 8787 Orion Place • Columbus, Ohio 43240-4027

www.MHKids.com

Printed in the United States of America.

1-57768-689-6 (HC)
1-57768-859-7 (PB)

Library of Congress Cataloging-in-Publication Data on file with the publisher.

1 2 3 4 5 6 7 8 9 PHXBK 07 06 05 04 03 02

 A Big Tuna Trading Company, LLC/J.R. Sansevere Book

YOU'RE THE SCAREDY-CAT
Written and illustrated by Mercer Mayer

Let's spend the night in
the backyard. If you're
not a scaredy-cat follow me!

We'll take pillows and blankets
and we'll take a flashlight...

just in case we need it.

We'll need a snack. You make the sandwiches.

I'll get the cake and lemonade.

We'll camp here.

Boy, oh boy! This is really great.

Do you want to hear a spooky story
about the green garbage can monster?

He's big and ugly and he creeps through
backyards and alleys looking for
garbage cans to eat. As a matter of fact,
he'll eat anything... even people!

Once upon a time a little boy
went camping in his backyard
and the next morning he was gone.
He disappeared without a trace.

The detective came and looked
around, but everyone knew
the green garbage can monster
had carried him away.

How about that!
Pretty scary story, huh?

I said... how about that?

Boy, you can't stay awake for *anything*.

It's just too noisy to sleep outside.
I think I'll go in.

You came in first,
so *you're* the scaredy-cat.